FUNNY FIRSTS ™

I'M DRACULA, WHO ARE YOU?

By Mike Thaler • Pictures by Jared Lee

Troll

**For
Tisha,**

Friend, friend, friend, and editor
M.T.

To
Les and Carolyn
J.L.

Text copyright © 1996 by Mike Thaler.
Illustrations copyright © 1996 by Jared Lee.
Published by Troll Communications L.L.C.
FUNNY FIRSTS™ is a trademark of Mike Thaler and Jared Lee.

Printed in the United States of America.

10 9 8 7 6 5 4 3 2 1

It's Halloween.

I'm going trick-or-treating . . .

ALONE . . .

for the first time!

I am going as
DRACULA.

Mom got me a
black cape and
fake fangs.

She got me a
trick-or-treat bag
and a flashlight.

I'm excited.
I'm scared, too.
Mom walks me
down the street.

It's dark.

Here come
FRANKENSTEIN and
the WOLFMAN.
I'm leaving!

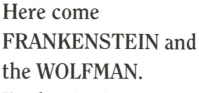

FRANKENSTEIN shouts,
"Wait!"
He comes up to me.
He's my best friend
Herbie.

The WOLFMAN comes up.
He's my second best friend Alfie.
He gave his sheepdog a haircut
and taped the fur on his face.

They say they're scared, too.
I say, "Just follow me."

We start up the steps
of the first house.
There's a grinning
jack-o'-lantern with
fire in its eyes.

Maybe we'll try the next house.

But there's a ghost floating on the porch.

And the next house has a giant spider.

This house looks okay.
Let's be brave.

We walk up the steps and ring the bell.

Mom comes to the door.
"Trick or treat!" we shout.
"Ohhh," says Mom. "It's Frankenstein!
And Wolfman!
And Dracula!"

"Yes," we say, sticking out our empty bags.
Mom fills them with coins and candy
and popcorn.

This is great! I'm not scared anymore.

We go back to the houses
with the jack-o'-lantern,

the ghost,

and the spider.

They give us lots of candy.

By then it's late, so I say good-night
to FRANKENSTEIN and the WOLFMAN.

I carry my treasures back home
and put them next to my bed.

I go to the sink and brush my fangs.

Then I wrap my cape around me
and slide under the blanket . . .

and dream of tomorrow's sweets.